WOOF
AND THE
BIG FIRE

by Danae Dobson

Illustrated by Karen Loccisano

WORD PUBLISHING
Dallas · London · Vancouver · Melbourne

This book is dedicated to the memory of my grandmother, Myrtle Dobson. A woman of great wisdom and love, the contribution she made to my life is a gift I can never repay.

Library of Congress Cataloging-in-Publication Data

Dobson, Danae.
    Woof and the big fire / by Danae Dobson ; illustrated by Karen Loccisano.
      p. cm. — (Read with me adventure series ; 7)
    Summary: When their dog risks his life to save three puppies from a burning house, Mark and Krissy are reminded of the sacrifice Jesus made for humanity.
    ISBN 0-8499-8362-2 : $6.99
    [1. Dogs — Fiction. 2. Fire fighters — Fiction. 3. Heroes — Fiction. 4. Christian life — Fiction.]
  I. Loccisano, Karen, ill.
  II. Title. III. Series.
PZ7.D6614Wos   1990
   [Fic] — dc20

90-33103
CIP
AC

Printed in the United States of America
01239AGH987654321

A MESSAGE FROM
Dr. James Dobson

Before you read about this dog named Woof perhaps you would like to know how these books came to be written. When my children, Danae and Ryan, were young, I often told them stories at bedtime. Many of those tales were about pet animals who were loved by people like those in our own family. Later, I created more stories while driving the children to school in our car pool. The kids began to fall in love with these pets, even though they existed only in our minds. I found out just how much they loved these animals when I made the mistake of telling them a story in which one of their favorite pets died. There were so many tears I had to bring him back to life!

These tales made a special impression on Danae. At the age of twelve, she decided to write her own book about her favorite animal, Woof, and see if Word Publishers would like to print it. She did, and they did, and in the process she became the youngest author in Word's history. Now, ten years later, Danae has written seven more, totally new adventures with Woof and the Petersons. And she is still Word's youngest author!

Danae has discovered a talent God has given her, and it all started with our family spending time together, talking about a dog and the two children who loved him. We hope that not only will you enjoy Woof's adventures but that you and your family will enjoy the time spent reading them together. Perhaps you also will discover a talent God has given you.

The hot sun beat down on the sidewalk as the Peterson children and their dog rounded the corner of Maple Street.

"Come on, Woof!" laughed Mark Peterson, pulling at the leash. "How many times do you have to stop?"

Woof paid no attention as he sniffed a nearby fire hydrant. He had stopped to smell every tree and bush along the way.

"Maybe we should go back home," suggested Krissy. "It's too hot out here."

"You're right," agreed Mark. "Let's go get some lemonade."

Just then, the children saw their friend, Fire Chief Jackson, walking toward them on the other side of the street. Two beautiful Dalmation dogs were walking beside him.

"Hello," he said as he came toward the children. "It's a little warm for a walk, wouldn't you say?"

"It sure is," said Mark. "Are those your dogs?"

"No," Chief Jackson answered. "The dogs' names are Spot and Speckles. They live at the fire station. I was taking them for a walk to get some exercise."

"This is our dog, Woof," said Mark.

"Well now," the fire chief laughed, "What kind of dog is *he*? He doesn't look like a purebred."

"No, Woof is just a mutt," said Mark, "but he's the smartest and best dog in the world."

"I see," Chief Jackson replied, looking down at Woof's bent ear and crooked tail. He wasn't convinced.

"Have there been any big fires in town lately?" asked Mark.

"No," said the Chief. "We've been lucky this summer. Everything has been pretty quiet. We've even had time to let neighborhood children visit the firehouse.

Then, his eyes brightened, and he said, "Hey, would you kids like to come visit the station? We would show you around and teach you a little about fighting fires."

"Wow!" squealed Krissy, "We'd *love* it!"

"Can we bring Woof?" asked Mark excitedly.

"Why, sure, bring him along," said the Chief. "I'll see you at my house next Saturday morning."

With that, he waved good-bye and walked away with the Dalmations at his side.

"Come on, let's go tell Mom and Dad," said Krissy.

When Mr. and Mrs. Peterson heard the news, they were delighted.

"Why, that sounds like a wonderful opportunity," said Father. "Chief Jackson has a great reputation in the city of Gladstone. Of course you may go."

When Saturday finally came, Mark and Krissy arrived at Chief Jackson's house. He met them at the door.

"Right on time," he said. "Let's be on our way, shall we?"

They all got in the front seat of Chief Jackson's pickup truck, with Woof riding in the back. Mark and Krissy could hardly believe their eyes when they reached the station. There were so many interesting things going on. Spot and Speckles were in the corner eating their breakfast, and there were several firemen busily working on the water hoses. The most exciting things they saw were two huge fire trucks parked in the garage! They were red and shiny.

Mark and Krissy jumped out of the pickup and followed Chief Jackson with Woof close behind. They were fascinated with all the equipment and the excitement going on around them. Some of the firemen slid down the poles while others polished the beautiful red fire trucks. When the men saw their boss, they stopped working and said hello.

"Boys, I want you to meet some friends of mine," said the Chief. "These are Mark and Krissy Peterson and their dog, Woof."

The firemen smiled and said "hi" to the children.

"Andy will give you a tour of the station while I get some coffee," said Chief Jackson.

The Peterson children shook hands with the fire chief's assistant.

"Would you like to sit behind the steering wheel of the biggest fire truck?" asked Andy.

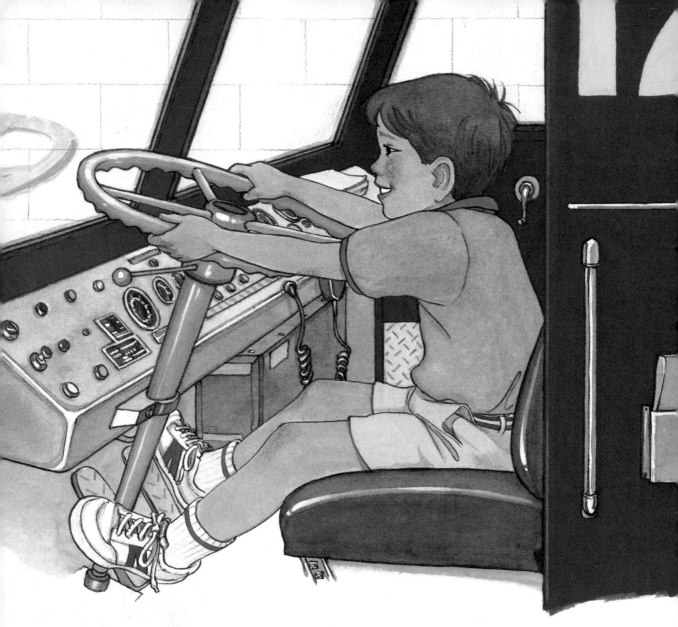

"Wow! Would I!" exclaimed Mark, climbing onto the driver's seat. Mark felt so big and important sitting in the fire truck. There was a shiny chrome siren on top and all sorts of fancy radio equipment beneath the dashboard. On each side of the truck were long wooden ladders, and there was a big fire hose behind the back seat.

"Firemen can get to any house in the city in less than five minutes," said Andy. "It doesn't matter what time of day or night. We're always ready to go."

"Don't you ever sleep?" asked Krissy.

"Sure, but we take turns going to bed. If the fire bell rings, we're up, dressed and down the fire pole in no time at all. That should allow you kids to sleep better, just knowing we're always on duty."

"Mark, I want to get up in the truck too," said Krissy, but just as she reached the front seat, a loud bell began to ring.

"Uh oh!" said Andy. "We have an emergency."

"Get down Krissy, Mark. We have to go."

The Peterson children quickly climbed off the truck and backed out of the way. Firemen began running in all directions putting on their coats and hats and jumping onto the truck. Chief Jackson headed toward the front with Spot and Speckles.

"Stay here with Andy," he said to the children. "We'll be back soon."

Mark and Krissy watched as the big truck pulled out of the driveway.

Suddenly, Krissy gasped, "Oh no! Where is Woof?"

They turned just in time to see a frightened Woof standing on the back of the fire engine as it sped away.

"There he goes!" yelled Krissy.

"What are we going to do?" asked Mark.

"Let's call Mom and Dad and see if they can help," she said.

Woof wasn't very happy about his situation either. The loud siren hurt his ears, and he struggled to stay on his feet as the fire engine swayed around corners. Still, no one on the truck had noticed he was there.

Very soon the firemen turned onto a side street and stopped in front of a burning house. They jumped out of the truck immediately and went to work. Some ran toward the house, while others hooked hoses to nearby fire hydrants.

Spot and Speckles were trained to stay in the truck so they would not be in the way.

Many neighbors had gathered around to watch as the flames shot through the roof.

Three firemen burst through the front door and ran through the house to make sure everyone was out. After finding no one inside, they quickly made a hole in the roof to let the smoke out. Then they ran outside to report that everyone was safe.

Just then, one of the firemen saw two children crying near the street.

"What's the matter?" he asked as he rushed over to them.

The two children rubbed their eyes and looked up at the fireman's kind face.

"There are three puppies trapped in the house," said the little girl. "The mother dog got out, but her babies are still inside."

"Is there anything you can do?" asked the boy, anxiously.

The fireman frowned and shook his head.

"No, I'm sorry," he said. "We can't risk a human life to save them, although I wish we could. The fire has become too dangerous for us to go back inside.

"But they're going to die!" the little girl sobbed.

"I'm sorry," said the fireman. "There's just nothing we can do."

Just then, Woof jumped off the truck and lifted his crooked ear! He had heard noises coming from the burning house! It was the sound of puppies yelping and whimpering.

GLADSTONE FIRE DEPT.

Dogs can often hear what humans can't, and Woof knew there was trouble in the house. Without wasting any time, he ran as fast as he could toward the front door. One of the firemen saw him dash into the house and yelled, "Stop!", but it was too late.

The two Dalmations danced and barked excitedly in the front seat of the truck. They had heard the puppies' cries too, but they were afraid to go near the smoky house.

Inside, Woof crawled from room to room looking from left to right. The smoke was so thick he could hardly breathe! It burned his eyes as he struggled to see where he was going.

Woof looked up and saw a heavy beam teetering above him. He jumped back just before it came crashing down in front of him.

He continued searching for the helpless puppies. Some-
times he had to crawl on his stomach to stay below the smoke.
The rooms became hotter as the tall flames licked
against the ceiling. Just when Woof was about to collapse
from the heat, he heard the puppies' cries again. The sound
seemed to be coming from the kitchen!

Woof followed the whines until he was near the puppies' bed. A burning cabinet fell with a crash near him, and a hundred dishes broke on the floor. Still, Woof struggled to reach the terrified puppies. He barked once to get their attention, and continued to crawl toward them, choking and coughing from the smoke.

Meanwhile, Mark and Krissy arrived at the fire with their parents. They had followed the smoke to find the right location. The children jumped out of the car and ran to one of the firemen.

"Have you seen our dog?" asked Mark anxiously, "He has shaggy hair and a crooked tail, and he accidently rode here on the fire truck."

"Yeah, I've seen the mutt. He ran into the house for some reason. I tried to stop him, but he kept right on going."

"Oh no!" cried Krissy. "Woof could die in there!"

"I hope he gets out alive!" Mark cried. "Why would he go into a burning house? Doesn't he know how dangerous it is?"

Woof knew about the fire, that's for sure! He was surrounded by it at the moment.

By crawling on his belly, Woof finally reached the puppies' bed. He grasped the smallest one by the loose skin on the back of its neck and carried it carefully in his mouth. The other puppies whimpered and followed Woof as he crawled out of the room and hurried through the smoke toward the living room. After what seemed like hours, they made it to the front door.

Exhausted, Woof staggered through the smoke onto the front porch. The puppy was still dangling from his mouth, and the other two waddled out behind him.

Mark and Krissy ran past the safety line to their dog. They threw their arms around him and patted his head. People in the crowd began cheering and clapping.

A local newspaper man snapped Woof's picture, and the firemen were *very* impressed! Everyone was proud of Woof, even Chief Jackson, who patted Woof's shaggy head.

"You were right, Krissy and Mark. This *is* a very special animal!"

The mother dog licked Woof's face in thanks for saving her little ones, while the two children cuddled the puppies. Woof was everyone's hero — the bravest and smartest dog of all!

The next day, Mr. Peterson brought the Sunday paper in and placed it on the table. There, on the front page was a picture of Woof with a puppy in his mouth! Mark and Krissy squealed with delight when they saw the photo. Mr. Peterson put on his eyeglasses and read the article that told about the fire and Woof's bravery. The newspaper said he was "braver than the dogs that belonged at the fire station" and called him "our favorite hero."

"Wasn't that an unselfish thing Woof did?" asked Krissy, reaching down to pat him on the head.

"It certainly was," said Father. "Woof cared more about saving the lives of the puppies than his own safety. He might have even died for them."

Suddenly, Mark thought of a scripture he had memorized in Sunday school.

"In John 15:13 Jesus said, 'The greatest love a person can show is to die for his friends.'"

"I'm glad you remembered that important verse," said Father. "It *does* have special meaning for us in this situation. Woof was willing to die for his little friends. But that scripture really tells about a much greater act of love. It has to do with our Heavenly Father loving us so much that He sent His only Son to die for us on a cross. That was the most wonderful thing ever done for people. Jesus died for His friends — and that includes you and me!"

"I think I understand that story even better, now," said Krissy.

"Me, too," agreed Mark.

Just then, the telephone rang. Mark answered the phone.

It was Chief Jackson calling from the fire station.

"Mark, this is Chief Jackson. All the men on the squad want to hang Woof's picture on the wall, and we'd like you to bring him down to receive an honorary medal."

"Thank you!" said Mark. "We're really proud of him."

"Oh, one other thing," said Chief Jackson. "We'd like to adopt Woof and make him our main fire dog. Do you think he'd like that?"

"Well," said Mark, "that's a big honor, but Woof is happy just being our good ol' family dog. I think he'd like to stay here with us."

Chief Jackson chuckled and said, "I understand."

When Mark hung up the phone, he told the rest of the family about the Chief's request.

"Dad, do you think Woof would rather belong to the firemen than to us?" asked Mark.

Mr. Peterson smiled. "Why don't you ask *him*?"

Mark knelt down by his dog and repeated the question. As if understanding every word, Woof suddenly knocked over Mark and Krissy and licked their faces.

"I think you have your answer," Mr. Peterson laughed.